SIMPLE PSI!

By F. L. WALL

He slipped on the jacket and scanned around the corner of the hall outside before he got to the door.

"I psi," whispered the pin in his lapel.

Egan Rains let go of the knob and felt for the emblem. It was inconspicuous, smaller than his thumbnail, the disc of the moon against a dark blue background. The markings delineated a face on the moon, and two radiating antennae.

Rains frowned and rolled it in his fingers. He thought he'd stripped himself of unnecessary identification. No harm done since no one in India had seen it on him, or heard it—yet. He looked at the emblem regretfully, turned it over. The back was inscribed: American Association of Psi Astronomers. It had sentimental value but he'd have to get rid of it.

He went to the disposer slot and dropped it into the wall. The insignia came whizzing back and struck the opposite wall. Muttering that foreign devices never worked the way they should, he dug it out. He examined it cursorily and noticed a tiny nick in the surface. That was all. The material was harder than the tough blades of the disposer. His respect for the techniques which made the pin mounted.

Someone walked by in the hall. Had the noise it made when it struck been heard? He let his mind reach out delicately.

"I pthi," grumbled the pin.

Now it was lisping—and it was louder. The blow must have damaged the speech crystals inside. Hurriedly he shut off his thoughts and the insignia responded with silence.

Primarily, it was a recognition device enabling people of the same talent, psimen, to identify each other. It served a purpose in America where there were so few, but in India, where mentalist activity was far greater, it was a handicap. It would be gabbling all the time.

Rains crumpled a sheet of paper around the little mechanism and tossed it gently into the chute. The disposer ground noisily and, as he half expected, the pin came hurtling back. He pried it out of the wall again. This time it was slightly bent.

"The disposer is for the convenience of guests. It's set to return all jewelry accidentally dropped into it."

Rains jumped and looked around wildly. He was certain there wasn't anyone in the room, and he hadn't observed a service screen. He still couldn't see either. But there was an eye staring at him from the wall.

"Shortages," explained the eye somberly, noting his bewilderment. "Our country doesn't yet produce all the material we need. Lacking full size tubes, the management of the hotel ordered smaller ones. They serve the purpose."

Only slightly larger than life, the eye blinked at him. It filled the entire screen. "If you must get rid of jewelry I suggest a pawnshop. It's more economical."

Rains glanced back with casual cageyness. How much had the other seen, or overheard? Probably nothing. He'd have noticed the eye. "Sorry. I was throwing an odd cuff link away."

"It was odd," conceded the eye. "A little harder and it wouldn't have come back." The eye blurred. "Can't have the disposer damaged, so we draw the line. If it's as hard as a diamond it passes through."

It was a convenient line and a profitable one, Rains noted absently as he went closer to observe the inconspicuous screen. Was it so tiny that it could have been on without his noticing?

"People don't throw away diamonds the way they used to," the eye complained.

Rains let him talk. This was something on which he had to reassure himself. And there was only one way to do it. The fellow was in a service department, somewhere in the distance. But Rains was certain he could reach him.

"I spy," said the pin, triggered by telepathy. "I spy."

The second trip to the disposer had damaged the crystals grievously. It had a vocabulary of two words and they never changed—but now they had. An outsider would get the wrong impression if he heard the distorted message. Rains clamped his fingers tighter on the emblem. But even that relatively slight pressure forced the speech crystals closer. "I spy," cried the pin. It seemed thunderous.

Simple psiman

F. L. Wallace

Alpha Editions

This edition published in 2023

ISBN : 9789357935531

Design and Setting By
Alpha Editions
www.alphaedis.com
Email - info@alphaedis.com

It took prolonged mental effort for Rains to remember that what he had to do was stop probing. The voice of the insignia was obligingly silent when he disengaged his mind.

The eye glared at him suspiciously. "You say something?"

"Not a thing."

"Didn't think so, unless you can talk without moving your lips." The eye disappeared and was followed on the screen by an unidentified lump of flesh, possibly a nose. Then the eye reappeared. Perhaps it was the other eye. "May have been tourist kids outside my window playing your favorite American game."

Rains nodded in relief. The voice had seemed loud to him but not to the other. His hands had smothered the reverberation. His nerves were merely on edge. "They love baseball," he said politely.

"Not baseball," said the eye. "I believe it had another name once, Hide and Seek. Now it's called I Spy." The eye blinked rapidly. "Well, so long."

When he was alone, Rains thought swiftly. His brief mental contact with the eye's mind convinced him he hadn't been observed in any suspicious act. That went to the credit side.

He felt the emblem. It was definitely not an asset. He thrust it determinedly into his pocket. He couldn't endanger his chances of finding the one man in India who meant so much to civilization and astronomy.

He rode down and went out of the hotel and onto the street. Momentarily, he wished he could go back. But the pin drove him past the long AFUA line.

In 1976 India was contradictory. In the last few decades it had achieved industrialization not much below Western standards. But it was densely populated and living patterns were not always equal to those of Europe and America. Rapid technical advances created new jobs and wiped them out again over night. A highly trained craftsman in the morning was often an unemployed vagabond by noon. Until he was taught new skills and could be reabsorbed back into the labor force he was an Applicant For Unofficial Aid. His dignity was such that he was never a beggar. Anyway, begging was forbidden by law.

Rains had no way of turning off his hearing. The best he could do was to walk swiftly and try to ignore the pleas. A few left their position in the AFUA line and trailed after him, but eventually they gave up and returned to the hotel to await other tourists.

It wasn't difficult for Rains to adopt the mannerisms of a sightseer. This was the vast motherland from which European languages and nations themselves had come in the remote past; complex, bewildering, containing the old while striving for the new. Cows in the streets imperiled jet cars and pedestrians. On the pinnacles of skyscrapers, holy men lay down on beds of nails while television cameras carried the picture to faithful followers in remote villages. Beside hydroponic gardens, fakirs mystified the curious with the ancient rope trick.

If his mission hadn't interfered, Rains would have liked to study these mentalists for his own satisfaction. He was a psiman himself, a powerful one, though of an elementary variety. He was a telepath, a man of one talent with no other ability—a simple psiman.

The emblem weighed as heavily in his pocket as it did in his mind. So far he hadn't found a quiet street on which to drop it. With so many people thronging the city, every city in India, it wasn't going to be easy. Nevertheless he wandered on, turning and twisting through boulevards and alleys until he came to the ideal place.

He slipped his hand in his pocket, jingling coins, and came out with the little talisman. He angled toward the curb and let it fall from his fingers. He relaxed mentally as soon as he was rid of it. Sweepers would brush it up and though it might attract another telepath's attention it couldn't be traced back to him.

He swerved to miss a cow that ambled down the street and smiled amiably. India was a romantic place, but it didn't conform to the highest standards of civilization.

A hand plucked at his elbow. "Pardon."

Rains turned. He recognized one of the men from the AFUA line. He'd been wrong; not all of them had become discouraged and gone back. Rains appraised him quickly, a squat fellow, not very tall, but he made up in width what he lacked in height. He wore a loin or ghandi cloth and a remarkably ugly turban. It was the usual attire for this part of India. His limbs, though not long, were of enormous muscular girth.

"I don't give alms," said Rains, tearing his gaze from the fascinatingly horrible turban. Passers by were staring at the man too.

The native's eyes held the impervious look of the unemployed. "I didn't ask, sir. You lost something." He held out his hand and the emblem was in it.

Rains snatched it in dismay. The native's face seemed innocent enough. Hesitating for only an instant, Rains made a quick mental stab, feigning a coughing spasm while he did so. "I psi, pthi, spy," bleated the pin. He jangled coins loudly and coughed harder.

Quickly he withdrew his mind. The Hindu didn't suspect a thing, though his eyes widened at Rains' impromptu performance. It didn't matter; he'd ascertained the other wasn't a telepath. Rains flipped a few coins toward him, said thanks and walked away.

He glanced back. The native was still trailing behind, evidently not satisfied with the reward. As long as the fellow was behind him, Rains didn't want to drop the emblem again. And he couldn't keep it.

Another idea came up. From the hotel he'd seen a stream winding through the city. It was yellow and muddy, an even better place for the disposal of the tricky little item. He angled off until he saw the river ahead, and noted that the native was still behind. He didn't want to go through that again!

His mind whirred smoothly as he stopped and bought gum. Chewing was not to his taste, but surmounting his dislike he peeled back the wrapper and thrust the stick in his mouth. He saved the wrapper and folded it over the emblem. As he crossed the bridge he tossed it, foil and all, into the river. Let it yammer away, sinking deeper in the mud or encysted in a crocodile's belly. Now it couldn't betray him.

But, in a way, it had. In his effort to get rid of the incriminating article he'd overlooked other things. There was a mind laying heavily against his. He struggled away, but for every retreat the intruder advanced.

It wasn't actually entering his thoughts. It stayed outside, gradually surrounding him. When had the invasion begun? He couldn't say with precision, but it couldn't have been long ago. It was a heavy mind, penetrating, not too acute. But it was endowed with brute strength and it was suggesting thoughts he didn't want to have.

For instance, he felt an intense desire to seek a shady spot beside a cool stream and lie down. Pleasantly textured grass would ease his skin and flies would buzz harmoniously near, tickling sensuously as they stung. Warm and moist. Fluid.

Rains was sweating. He had to shake off this insidious attack.

First, he had to locate the source. Not the AFUA beggar. He was near, but Rains had already ascertained he wasn't a telepath. The street was now crowded with men and beasts. That was the trouble; there was no easy way to pick out his assailant.

Which one? Rains glanced around. The white bearded ascetic next to him? He was the holy hermit, telepathic type. But so were dozens of others, most of them with luxuriant white beards. Rains probed, but got no results.

In America he'd fenced off combined telepathic assaults of the best of his fellows. He'd expected more competition in India, but this was beyond his expectation. The defense he'd prepared seemed weak for what it had to ward off.

An olive-skinned, dark-eyed girl went by with a gliding graceful walk. With a little help from his imagination he could conjecture every curve. It was sufficiently distracting. Me plus thee equals whee, he thought swiftly. But this is hardly a Euclidean proposition, though I would like our parallel paths to meet.

Was he too hopeful, or did the surrounding thoughts retreat somewhat? The girl turned and retraced her steps. Me plus thee equals three, her reply came back firmly. What do you have in mind?

She wasn't thinking along the right lines. There was a mental wedding scene uncomfortably close. He went on, ignoring her opportunistic suggestion.

I should have known, she thought frozenly when he didn't respond. You're looking for another kind of girl. She took herself out of the picture.

It was dangerous to spread his thoughts around. Something less personal was in order. Nonsense was reputed to work. He searched and found some, repeating it silently. I was thinking of a plan to dye my whiskers green, and always wear so large a fan they never could be seen.

An ascetic, there seemed to be hundreds around, walked by. I was thinking of a plan—continued Rains, his effort intense—to dye my whiskers green....

The ascetic bellowed as a cow butted his side and began munching his beard. A green beard! The Hindu squirmed and twisted loose, backing away from the cow. The cow lollopped out her tongue and tucked a whisp of beard into her mouth, chewing away as if on grass, which it resembled. Purposefully she advanced.

The old Hindu scrambled away, clutching the remains of his beard. It was now green, but it had been white. Rains could swear he had been looking at it during the instant of change. The cow lurched after the old man. She broke into a trot and the trot stretched into a gallop and the two of them disappeared down the street.

All around there were men with green beards. It wasn't natural. They stared at each other and then their eyes glided down. Muttering in foreign tongues they stalked away. Rains could understand their consternation. What had caused their beards to change? Did it have anything to do with the rhyme?

But there was something more important. The mind that had been trying to invade his had gone away. He thought back. The mental influence had vanished with the cow.

An animal telepath? In India it wasn't totally unexpected. It was the reason he was here. And the thoughts were those a cow would have—internal evidence couldn't be ignored. It was frightening that the cow was a stronger telepath than he, but it was also a source of relief. At least the animal hadn't filched any secrets from him.

He had another conclusion to allay his anxiety. The girl he'd mentally whistled at had been able to intercept his thoughts. Learning that he wasn't interested in what she wanted, she had politely if frigidly withdrawn. Mental courtesy? Well, why not?

Even in India there weren't many telepaths, say one in five or ten thousand. But considering the density of population, that was a lot. They had to evolve a code of mental conduct or life would be intolerable. No one violated another's thoughts except for good reason. If he watched himself, Rains thought, he'd have no cause for alarm. No one would snatch his plans from his mind.

Rains walked on, wondering who or what had changed the white beards to green. A powerful mind at work, but not the cow; he was certain of this. Nor the girl.

Rains fished discreetly about. Not the least hint. But the nonsense rhyme had influenced someone, and that person was now lost to him.

If he'd had the time, Rains would have liked to find and study the unusual man who'd saved him with that green beard trick. An unorthodox talent, limited but interesting. After the menace that hung far out in space was ended, he would come back and search out his unseen benefactor.

Regretfully Rains cancelled these interesting thoughts, and looked around for his indefatigable AFUA follower. The man was gone, despairing at last of wheedling more alms. Or perhaps he'd been frightened by the strange occurrence on the street.

Rains wandered back to the hotel. Upon approaching it he stopped. The AFUA line had grown longer, curling around the block, ending almost where it began. It wouldn't help to go to the back entrance, because the line was there too.

Rains lowered his head and plunged on toward the front entrance. A hand touched his elbow. "Guide?" inquired a voice. Someone asking for work, not money, was unusual.

The voice was faintly familiar. Rains swung around. It was the man who'd handed back the emblem. For this Rains owed him nothing. And yet he did. Because of this he'd been forced to find a better means of disposing of it.

He did need a guide, but he hadn't intended to hire one until he got to Benares, far to the north, where he hoped his search would end. The man he had to find was completely unknown, and Rains had only faint clues to go on, so he'd have to rely on his telepathic power to uncover more information.

Rains beckoned and the man stepped out of the AFUA line, no recognition in his eyes. "Let's see your license," Rains said. The man fumbled in his turban and produced it.

Rains read silently, "Experience one year." Too bad. His mission couldn't be trusted to a beginner. "I'll think about it," he said, handing back the card. "If you don't find anything else, be here tomorrow. I may come out." Tomorrow he'd be on his way to Benares.

The native folded the license into his turban and went back. He was now at the very end of the line because he'd left his place to follow Rains. He'd get little tossed to him today, and the coins Rains had given him wouldn't buy much. Rains could sense despair.

Rains beckoned him back. "Do you have any other skills that might be useful?" he asked. "What did you do before you became a guide?"

The eyes brightened, then faded in quick defeat. "Nothing you'd want," he mumbled. "For ten years I was a dyeman."

Rains thought back to the scene of the mental ambush. Beards. Green beards. The dyeman had been near at the time.

"Dyeman?" he repeated, trying to keep the excitement out of his voice. Even if it actually had taken place as he thought, it was only a minor talent. But there was always empathy between psipeople, even though their abilities might be unrelated. He could expect closer cooperation from this man than from any other guide he might hire.

"I may be able to use you," he said. "Come in. We'll talk." He'd discovered a new field for Rhine investigation. They'd mention it in history books, after they described how he saved the world.

Gowru Chandit accepted the drink gratefully. Rains leaned back and said, "Is this what you're trying to say? You first noticed your ability when the dye didn't arrive at the textile factory. You had a quota to meet. In panic you ran the cloth through anyway, and it came out the color you wanted."

Gowru nodded.

"Can you tell me how you do it?"

The Hindu looped his hand near his head and shrugged.

Rains nodded. Any other answer would have been surprising. "What did they say at the factory when you told them?"

Gowru grinned slyly. "Alas, I'm a poor man. I didn't tell them."

Rains could follow the man's thoughts as long as they were composed in English. Alloted chemicals, Gowru smuggled everything out of the plant that wasn't used and sold it to other firms. It should have been profitable. "Why aren't you still with them?" Actually he knew the answer. A new process had displaced the dyeman.

"I soon became foreman of the entire plant. I alone had charge of all coloring. I was wildly prosperous, what with one thing and another. It was my downfall."

"I don't understand." He did, but it was best to lead the man on, to explore all possibilities.

"I drank," said Gowru. "I had money for it and I drank too much."

"And lost your ability?"

"It was not so simple," said Gowru. "No, my ability became stronger than ever." He meditated briefly. "Picture me, the master dyeman who alone colors all the material that passes through the plant. So skillful am I, so beautiful the colors that the poorest cloth becomes transfigured and commands premium prices.

"I arrive at work one morning and I am sick. I go into my secret mixing room and lose my breakfast there. My head throbs. I raise it and look at the chart. So much green, so much red and yellow, so much everything.

"The chemicals are there and I put them into the suitcase which the management graciously allows me to take in and out of the factory. The pipes which fill the various vats flow through this room. As I have always done, I concentrate on the wanted colors, associating them with the proper vats. But my head hurts, you understand. Alternately, it grows large and small in defiance of the laws of physics."

Gowru Chandit paused to shake his head sorrowfully in remembrance of that day. "I concentrate until all the vats are filled and then, as usual, go to sleep. All day the automatic machinery hums. Yards pass through the vats, bolt after bolt is dyed, dried and wound, and nobody looks because this operation is automatic.

"Then, the manager comes to inspect production and rub his hands at the profits that will accrue to him. He unwinds a sample, looks at it and screams." Gowru stared mournfully at Rains. "Retroactive to that scream I am fired."

"But why?"

Gowru loosened a fold of his turban and spread it out so the pattern was visible. "I was projecting. Did you ever see such a headache reproduced in full color? Not merely a headache, but also a hangover."

Rains moved the drink hastily away. He wanted to speak, but it might be dangerous to open his mouth. The crisis passed. "Put it away!" But Gowru had already refolded it so that the pattern was no longer discernible. The cloth was an unpleasant souvenir.

Egan Rains was silent, studying the Hindu. The man was honest and loyal, that much he could tell. But though he spoke English well, he didn't think extensively in it and most of his thoughts were hidden in a language Rains couldn't translate, mentally or otherwise. "Can you teleport?" he asked.

"A mind carrier?" said Gowru. "No, I'm only a dyeman. I can do nothing else."

He expected that; there weren't many who had multiple powers. "Do you know anyone who can?"

"I have a friend who plays ping pong with it."

That was telekinetics, not teleportation, but it might be what he was after. So far as the Rhine Institute knew, people with either ability existed only in India. "How good is your friend?" he asked.

"At ping pong, very good. At tennis, poor. The ball is too heavy; he can't move it fast enough."

Then that was a false lead. The person he wanted had to be much more adept and powerful. Rains would have to look farther and Gowru would have to help him. "Gowru, I'm an astronomer," he began.

The Hindu raised his eyebrows to express interest. "I've always had a soft spot in my head for astronomy," he declared.

Evidently the idiom did change from country to country. "My colleagues and I at Palomar have discovered a new comet," he went on. "It is a strange comet, bigger than most, almost a tiny planet. The composition is stranger still, mostly oxygen and water."

Gowru nodded sagely. "And you want me to color the water. That I can do, any hue you want. But if there is much air and you want me to color that too, you will have to be satisfied with a light tint, a pale blue or green or pink."

"The color doesn't matter," said Rains gravely, and poured himself another drink. "In seventeen years that comet is due to strike Earth."

The Hindu bowed his head. "I've had a feeling of doom since you mentioned the comet," he said simply.

"Wrong," said Rains. "No doom. In seventeen years we'll have rockets that can meet it out in space. We'll load hydrogen bombs into rockets and blow the comet into fine crystals. But the orbit of the particles will still intersect that of Earth, and it will fall as rain."

Gowru searched his memory for a foreign concept. "Forty days and forty nights?"

"I don't know how long," said Rains wearily. "But whatever happens, the water level of the oceans will rise—from fifty to three hundred feet is the present estimate. After we study it longer we'll know exactly. The land area will shrink, but that alone isn't disastrous. Forewarned, not many lives would be lost. Most people will have time to move to higher ground.

"However, there's another aspect. Air is also present in the comet and will be added to our atmosphere. The earth will grow warmer and the higher latitudes will become habitable. Perhaps we'll gain almost as much living space as we lose."

"Then let's rejoice," said Gowru, reaching for the bottle. "It's not every comet which is so considerate."

Rains replenished his own glass. "It's not an occasion for rejoicing. We've calculated that, with the additional atmosphere and moisture, astronomy will become extinct. Cloud covered, the planet will be much like Venus. No one will be able to see the stars." He didn't mention that a few of the highest mountains would still rise above the clouds. He didn't because those mountains were in India and that country would then have a monopoly on the science.

Gowru wrinkled his face in pleasure at the whisky and then assumed a properly doleful expression. "I see. In seventeen years you'll be unemployed." He added consolingly. "Maybe they'll give you a pension."

Rains' vision was growing a little fuzzy, but his intellectual goals had not changed. "It's not the pension," he said irritably. "I intend to save astronomy."

"It's not reasonable to be so obstinate when the heavens decree otherwise," declared Gowru. "You should cultivate an interest in other things. Girls are a nice hobby."

Rains muttered something about girls and Gowru interrupted.

"Good. We can start with girls and there's no telling where we'll end. I'm a guide and I can help in such matters. How many do you want?"

"I've only a normal—"

Again Gowru interrupted. "I was afraid of that—only a normal interest in girls. You should moderate your desires. I can't help you with so many." He shook his head sadly. "Let's get back to astronomy."

"I expect to," said Rains coldly. "As I was saying, at Palomar we have the giant telescope—"

"The big inch," said Gowru fondly.

"You're thinking of something else," said Rains. "In addition to the big telescope we have a secret instrument not duplicated nor imagined elsewhere—a psiscope." Thoughtfully he poured the remaining whisky into his glass.

"Don't ask me how it works. It's designed for use by people of psi powers, of which I'm one. It's incredibly powerful and accurate. With it we've learned things that other astronomers won't know for several years. The data on the comet is one example."

He raised the glass and let the liquid trickle down his throat. "We've also learned things that astronomers with conventional instruments will never find out—that there are teleports in India."

Gowru struggled with himself, and decided to hoard the whisky in his glass. He sipped delicately at it. "I could have told you that and I don't have a psiscope. But how did you find out?"

"Imagine the comet swinging nearer the sun. Under the terrific radiation, the frozen ball of water melts and the atmosphere expands. In our psiscope, clearly illuminated, is an object no one else can see at that distance. It is a peculiar object, man made, and found only in one place on Earth." He paused. "At present we don't have a rocket capable of going to the moon. And yet this object was transported much farther. Therefore, it had to be teleported there."

"Logical," agreed Gowru. "What was this object?"

"I can tell you the city from which it came; you'll have to know anyway— Benares. But my colleagues and I have decided we can't tell anyone what it was we saw on the comet."

"Benares," mused the Hindu. "I know the city well. I was there last year looking for work."

"With your help," said Rains, "we intend to contact this teleport."

"Who's we?"

"My colleagues and I at Palomar."

"And also your government?"

"Our government doesn't enter into this. We couldn't convince them if we tried since they don't believe in psi powers. No, this is solely our problem. We're financed in part by the Rhine Institute and we have other funds which were diverted for the purpose."

Gowru sighed. No matter which way he tilted it, there wasn't another drop in his glass. "What are you going to do with this teleport after you find him?"

"Persuade him to come to the United States. We'll get him out of India some way." The country wouldn't take kindly to an attempt to smuggle out one of their mentalists, but it could be done.

"What good will that do?" questioned Gowru. "Even the most experienced teleport can't change the path of the comet. It's too big to move."

"He won't have to move it," said Rains. "We've positive proof that he did transport a—uh—large object to the comet. He did it once and he can do it again, except this time it will be a hydrogen bomb."

"I thought so," said the Hindu disgustedly. "I don't want any part of it. Where will you get that hydrogen bomb except from your government? Let them develop their own teleports, or approach our country through proper diplomatic channels."

"You're not thinking," said Rains. "With a teleport working for us we don't ask the army for a hydrogen bomb. One minute they have it safely hidden, and the next instant it's inside the comet. Let the military boys worry about how it got away and where it went.

"You see, the comet's been captured by the sun and moves in a very eccentric orbit just inside Jupiter. If we vaporize it now, it will lose most of its mass to those two bodies. There'll be little left to fall on Earth." He nodded approvingly to himself. The plan would be effective, if he found the teleport.

Gowru's eyes expanded, enlarged by his own inner fires. "Let's drink to it," he said, extending his glass.

Rains sighed. As a secret agent he needed an analytically clear mind at all times. But he also had to have someone who understood India better than any American could, someone who would work with him wholeheartedly. It wouldn't pay to offend such a person. He opened a bottle, and later, still another....

The train wound through the provinces and cities en route—Bangalore, Jubbulpore, Jetadore, finally arriving at Benares. They could have gone more conveniently by air, every sensible Indian did, but presumably it was worth something to maintain the pose of tourist and guide.

From the window of his hotel Rains could see the Ganges, a muddy, sluggish river still, but an improvement over what it had been thirty years before. More sanitary too; burial customs could not be completely changed in a generation, but the three phoenix barges anchored off shore automatically disposed of the bodies to the satisfaction of all but the most fanatic.

Southward were the spires of a rather shabby building he could identify from photographs, the Rhine Institute of the Ganges. Its value was dubious, of missionary rather than research caliber. In the heart of the mentalist country, it had little prestige and not much more patronage. It was questionable who spied most on the other, the American staff or the supposed native converts. Each side took precautions, but there were startlingly few devices which were effective against an accomplished telepath.

Still, mechanical devices partly reduced the advantages of the Indians. Chewing gum parked in the right places often concealed ingenious mechanisms, and even the birds which were regularly fed at the Institute sometimes swallowed grain-sized instruments which were carried impartially to all the public buildings of the city.

This didn't concern Rains. The Rhine Institute of the Ganges could solve its own problems or fail to do so. But somewhere in Benares there was a teleport. Where?

The regular reports—coded, scrambled, shielded, unshielded, unscrambled, decoded—had mentioned great mentalist activity, but hadn't been able to pin it down. Fakirs and holy men abounded; there were at least a dozen telepaths in the city better than Rains, not to mention clairvoyants.

Communication from the Institute had always been erratic, understandable in view of the hazards. Rains had not seen a report from this branch in three months. Perhaps in the interim they had uncovered more information. He would have to find out. "Gowru," he asked, "are there many fogs in Benares?"

The Hindu wrinkled his face in thought. "I've been here when there were. Not now though; wrong time of the year."

That was not good. Rains didn't want to expose himself, but he had to get in touch with the director of the Institute.

"If you want a fog, I'll get you one," said Gowru.

Rains glanced up. The Hindu was a queer fellow. Rains had dismissed the talk of coloring the comet's atmosphere as drunken boasting, but what if it wasn't?

"Can you actually create fog?" he asked doubtfully.

"Sure. Want a sample?"

Perhaps he should, but too many fogs at this time would be suspicious. He shook his head, "If you say you can deliver, I believe you. The only question is, can you cover most of the city?"

"The whole northern part of India," Gowru assured him.

"That much won't be necessary. How long can you hold it?"

"Depends on the wind," said his guide, extending his thumb and forefinger and rubbing them together delicately. "Air's slippery stuff. It fades. I'll have to concentrate."

Rains sighed. He'd learned that when Gowru concentrated he had to be diluted. He set out a bottle....

Rains walked along the bank of the Ganges and glanced at his watch. An hour to sunset. The fog was due at any moment. The Institute was a few blocks away, but he had memorized a map of the area and would be able to get there no matter what happened.

He adjusted his tie in a mirror. No one behind him, but he didn't think they'd be that crude about it here. He practised shutting off his thoughts. His defense was adequate in America, but he wasn't sure how effective it would be against a first rate Indian mentalist.

He went into a curio shop and picked up a small bronze statue of a four-armed god. He was about to pay for it when the woman behind the counter shrieked. He glanced up at her. She was merely a few feet away, but he could scarcely see her through the thick black smoke that curled through the room.

"Fire!" screamed the woman and ran out.

He hurried to the door and then thought of the statue in his hands. It wouldn't do to get involved in a petty theft charge. He ran back to the counter and laid the money down. On second thought he left the statue there too and stumbled out of the shop.

The street was jammed. Storekeepers stood on the curb and shouted, and out of the buildings thick smoke came pouring. Rains sniffed. It looked like smoke but had no smell. He thought he knew what it was. This was the fog Gowru had said he would create.

It was a good fog but it was placed wrong—inside buildings instead of filling the free air overhead. It had the opposite effect from what he wanted. He had expected to approach the Institute through dim and shrouded streets. As it was, he had to elbow people into the gutter in order to move. Fire sirens wailed in a dozen directions and spotting copters took to the air and started circling around.

"Gowru!" he thought sharply, but either the distance was too great or his thoughts were swallowed up by the multitude around him. Contact was impossible.

He'd have to do the best he could; confusion might cover him. A fire truck skidded to a stop beside him and frantic firemen coupled the hoses and went to work. Drenched and swearing Rains fought his way down the street.

As abruptly as it began, the smoke stopped. At least the drunken Gowru had had enough sense to look out the window. Or maybe the sirens had brought him around. Rains shuddered; he could almost see the contents of the bottle diminishing as Gowru apprised himself of the mistake.

He was a block or so from the Institute and the streets were still crowded. Some people had re-entered the stores as soon as the smoke-like stuff stopped pouring out. Others, more fearful, remained outside.

They didn't remain outside long. Overhead, in the sunset sky, an ominous cloud formed. It descended rapidly upon the city. Apprehensively, Rains watched the copters disappear into the dense cloud, and then decided against worrying about them. Radar equipped, they could trace their way through anything.

Shopkeepers gazed at the sky, shuddered, and hurried inside. They closed windows and doors and bolted them. The reason escaped him until he observed firemen clambering into trucks which roared away as fast as they had come. They wore masks, all of them. It was gas they feared.

The fool was compounding the mistake. A quiet, ordinary fog which gathered inconspicuously in the hollows and low places and gradually engulfed the city was what he wanted. This sort of thing was hardly what he had specified.

There was no help for it, and as long as he had the streets to himself he might as well go ahead. Before he reached the Institute the fog fell on him with an almost physical impact. Streetlights winked on briefly and were snuffed out as the fog descended lower, still burning but not discernible at street level.

He shuffled slowly along, touching buildings. This kept him from getting completely lost. There was no one following him physically, he was sure of that. They could still keep track of him mentally and he wouldn't be aware of it, but he doubted that anyone was interested in him at a time like this. They'd be too concerned with the fog.

The dyeman was good—too good.

He stopped at a doorway, pressing his face close to the glass to read the sign on it. It was the Institute, but he didn't intend to enter.

He stepped back from the door and squeezed behind a statue. He was as close to the director as he could expect to get without being observed by the spies on the staff. Telepathically he located the director's office and whispered, also telepathically. There was no reply.

It took him a minute to determine why—the director was asleep. It was better that way. The man wouldn't know he had come, taken the information and left. He stirred around in the sleeping mind, delicately so as not to awaken him. Then he had the information.

Gommaf was the man he wanted. Rains grinned to himself. Gommaf was the teleport, or knew who the teleport was—he couldn't be sure which. That was all he needed.

He wriggled out from behind the statue and walked quickly away. The fog wasn't as intense as it had been, though it slowed him considerably. Gowru must be getting tired. Streetlights were burning faintly overhead.

The fog changed color as he went along, an indiscreet slip. There was a slight brown tinge to it that wasn't altogether pleasant. He walked faster and his stomach felt upset.

Gowru was playing with the fog; that was the only interpretation Rains could place on it. Colors shifted through the spectrum. He wished the Hindu would stop it. A queasy, dirty violet didn't inspire confidence in his own digestive system.

In the midst of all that violet, a low-flying biliously pink cloud came toward him. He turned his head and gulped, but it didn't help appreciably. In the direction he now faced there was a vile green fog shape. It looked something like an appendix, but it was much larger.

He was wrong. Gowru Chandit was not playing—this was for keeps. A valuable man, no doubt of it, but he drank too fast and couldn't control his reactions.

As he looked, the appendix shape writhed slowly and glowed. Other fog forms began materializing convulsively around him, not all of them bearing morphological resemblance to human organs, but not necessarily of more pleasing appearance because of that. And the colors—Rains closed his eyes but the damnable fluorescence seemed to penetrate.

The river was nearby, for which he was thankful. He staggered to it, lay down on the embankment, and retched feebly. The Ganges below became less sanitary for a time. There were certain disadvantages to psi powers, he reflected. This was the first time he had reacted to another's nausea.

Later, he made it back to his quarters.

———————————

The boat slid swiftly and smoothly past the cremation barges anchored in the river. The design of the barges was distinctive, two long cylindrical pontoons connected fore and aft by beams which curved above the surface of the water. In the middle of each pontoon was a squat affair resembling a searchlight, each of which was focused inward toward the open space at the center of the barge. Upstream was a long line of small wooden rafts. One at a time they were allowed to float between the pontoons. The searchlights flashed and the beams crossed in the center. The raft burst into flame, water boiled for an instant, and the corpse was utterly consumed. The barge was ready for the next body.

Rains glanced at the mechanism. No matter where he saw it, he'd always be able to identify it. One of them was much newer than the others. This was significant.

Gowru was scowling, so Rains refrained from mentioning the barges. There were many religions in India, now more than ever, and each had its own burial customs. Some rituals were offensive to other sects and he saw no need to antagonize his guide over such a trivial matter.

They were both silent as the boat pulled up to the civic center pier. Government offices and allied functions were situated together in an annex outside the city proper; a sensible solution in a city as ancient as Benares, but one which Rains did not particularly like. There were just too many policemen and security officers around. He shrugged. That was probably the least of his problems.

They mingled with the crowd, sightseers and officeworkers, that rushed off the ship. In a few minutes they were in the center of the government city. Police everywhere, but Rains didn't let that bother him. Presently they came to an impressive building and he stood on the sidewalk and pretended to admire it.

There were heavily barred windows and guards at the entrance. "Here it is," he said softly. "We could walk in."

"This is just Gojmaf," grunted Gowru. "Mere journeymen. You want the Guild of Master Mystics Mentalists and Fakirs—Gommaf."

Rains sighed; he'd not been as fortunate as he'd thought in contacting the sleeping director's mind. He'd not gotten the name of the teleport, but the organization to which that person probably belonged.

The Gommaf building was on another street and wasn't easily located, but they found it. They sat at a sidewalk cafe and inspected it from a distance. It was not a pretentious structure and there were neither bars nor guards.

The absence of visible security measures was disturbing. It suggested several possibilities: that there was nothing of value inside, that Gommaf had complete confidence in the ordinary police patrol, or that they relied on other means of protection. The last seemed likely.

It was a local organization and Rains had never heard of it. That was not strange. There was much about India that had never reached the Western world. There were records inside, the records of a teleport, and he had to get to them.

He couldn't just walk in; somewhere there was a master telepath on duty. Rains had confidence in his own ability, but he saw no point in overmatching himself. "What do you know about Gommaf?" he asked.

His guide looked at the tea with less than delight. "It's fairly new," he said slowly, searching his memory. "Organized about ten years ago, I believe. There was competition at first. Some of the mystics, mentalists and fakirs thought they were outside the orbit of ordinary trade unionism. They formed a rival organization and tried to eliminate Gommaf's chief organizer, a man called Handas Bvandeghat. They found him one morning while he was practising yoga, and of course he refused to interrupt his spiritual contemplation. They riddled him with machine gun bullets."

Rains nodded. "But they couldn't kill the idea. Handas Bvandeghat became a martyr and the organization went on in spite of, or because of, his death." It was a familiar story.

"Who said he died? Handas Bvandeghat is president of Gommaf."

"But they machine gunned him!"

"Sure, they shot him. But he's a fakir, still makes a living letting people drive spikes through his body. What's a few bullets to him?" Gowru swallowed the tea and made a face. "Of course, there were some physical consequences. Even today Bvandeghat has trouble keeping food on his stomach." Gowru wiped his mouth with the back of his hand. "Holes," he added.

It was not such a familiar story after all, but it did emphasize the difficulties. An organization headed by such a character would be tough. The telepath to spot intruders, which had previously been merely a possibility, became a certainty. An approach to the front entrance was inadvisable.

But the comet was still hurtling through space and the only man who could avert the collision was the teleport. Rains had to contact him. He produced a map and consulted with his guide. After some discussion they evolved a plan.

"If we come through the rear it's your opinion the telepath won't detect us?" Gowru murmured, obviously doubtful.

"It's worth trying," said Rains, folding the map. "Behind the Gommaf building is an electric fence and behind that is open country, mostly swamp. Normally the swamp is considered impassable, but there is a way through it. The telepath has to concentrate mentally just as you do visually. He'll be expecting trouble from the front. I sneak in from the rear, examine the records, and get out again before it occurs to him that I've been there. After that I still have to contact the teleport, but once I know who he is, that's easy."

"Why not rent a copter and set it down in the middle of the swamp? It will save a lot of walking."

"It would, but it would also inform Gommaf that we're up to something. No, we'll just have to walk." Rains stuffed the map into his pocket. "Are there any shrines on the road to the city?"

Gowru Chandit shrugged. "There are shrines anywhere in India except straight up."

Rains nodded with great satisfaction. There'd be one there too when the hydrogen bomb exploded inside the comet. A bright flaring shrine to astronomy.

The road was paved but dusty. There were other tourists walking toward the city so Egan Rains and Gowru were by no means conspicuous. At some distance from the civic center they stopped at a wayside temple. They entered and examined the strange but not notable architecture, the intricate but not always esthetically pleasing carved walls. When they were not observed they slipped through a side door and hurried to the rear where they plunged into the light underbrush. In half an hour they were at the edge of an open plain. No one followed them.

After some discussion they decided to skirt the plain, and started out, keeping well within the shadow of the trees which separated plain from adjacent swampland. They circled back toward the civic center, toward the narrow spot of firm ground that reached nearly to the electric fence behind Gommaf. In the middle of the afternoon they rested and ate some of the food they had brought with them.

"Psst!" said Gowru, waving his great hand.

Rains swallowed. "I don't hear anything."

Again the Hindu flapped his hand for silence. After listening intently, he crawled away into the underbrush. Presently he came back. "Soldiers," he whispered.

Rains was worried. Did that mean Gommaf knew what he was up to? And if so, why did they send out soldiers? He could swear no one had tapped his mind. "How many?" he asked in a low voice.

"Thousands."

Allowing for exaggeration, there were still too many. He picked up the sandwiches, shoving one in his mouth and the rest into his pocket. "Let's go," he said.

"Where?"

He pointed in the direction they'd been heading.

Gowru shook his head. "They're coming from there too."

That made it difficult. He looked questioningly at the swamp, but his guide frowned. "Snakes," he said laconically. "Tigers, crocodiles."

That left the plain, but out there they'd be spotted instantly, and picked up soon after. He couldn't afford to be questioned by anyone. He could hear the soldiers. They were getting closer.

The plain. They had to cross it and yet they couldn't. Unless—He turned to Gowru. "A fog," he said triumphantly. "All we need is another fog."

His guide smiled with sorrowful dignity. "It takes whisky to make a good fog. If you had listened to me you would have brought a supply along. But alas, you are the reformer type, and because of that we are now caught." His head sunk forward in defeat.

His chin touched his chest and at that his head snapped back and it was easy to see that he was not defeated. "Without whisky I can't make a fog," he admitted. "Do you know how many molecules are involved in even a medium-sized fog?"

Rains didn't, but thought he ought to look impressed.

"A surface now, even a relatively large surface, contains a comprehensible number of molecules," said Gowru. "My mind isn't sharp when I'm sober, but I can handle that many."

"I don't see how—" But darkness interrupted his thoughts. "What is that?" asked Rains.

"I put a surface around us. It has the shape of a tank."

It was surprisingly sensible. There were two groups of soldiers approaching along the edge of the swamp, and they were in the middle. It was logical to assume that one group of soldiers would consider the so-called tank as belonging to the other.

His eyes were adjusting to the changed light: he could see dimly through the outline that surrounded them. A hundred yards away a soldier appeared through the trees, saw the tank and stopped. Rains didn't like the way he fingered the rifle.

"Can you move this thing?" he asked nervously.

"Why not?"

"Good. Let's get away from here."

It weighed little more than nothing—as insubstantial as air. It was air, bound together on a molecular level by forces originating in the Hindu's mind. It moved out on the plain as fast as they could walk.

"Halt!" a voice rang out from the edge of the swamp.

"Let them try to stop us," whispered Gowru cheerfully.

Again the voice commanded, but Gowru paid no attention. A rifle shot sounded behind them and a bullet whizzed uncomfortably close. "Maybe we'd better stop," suggested Rains.

"A Chandit never surrenders," said his guide stubbornly. Abruptly the darkness around them deepened. Another rifle shot rang out. The bullet struck the tank shape, and glanced away.

Air did that, or more correctly, the psi forces of his guide's mind. He had grossly underestimated the man. "How did you do that?"

"Increased the thickness of the surface by a few molecules," said Gowru cheerfully. "Handy, if you know how."

It was handy, but there were also disadvantages. No light at all entered and they couldn't see where they were going.

Rains thought swiftly. Perhaps he could use the soldiers to guide him. His mind reached out, and was bent backward. Ten inches of steel couldn't stop his thoughts, but a few molecules of air did. The man had limited ability, but was exceedingly powerful within those limitations. He explained the difficulty to Gowru, who stopped and scratched his head.

"If I made a tiny hole—"

"That's all I need," said Rains, and his mind was through it as it formed. He skipped from thought to thought, lightly so as not to leave an awareness of his mental presence. The two groups of soldiers had joined and started after them, cautiously and at a safe distance.

Unwittingly he and Gowru had stumbled into army maneuvers. And it wasn't going to be easy to get out of them. Naturally, the soldiers were curious. And the tank—He looked into the lieutenant's mind.

He shivered. There weren't supposed to be tanks in this area. And Gowru was not an army man; his idea of a tank was different from that of Indian designers. He had created a fearsome image, the more frightening because it didn't correspond to any known make, friendly or foreign. This was something the Army was going to investigate, with everything they had.

He explained it briefly to his guide.

"Hmmm," said Gowru. "Maybe I should change the shape to something they're familiar with?"

He'd thought of that. "It's too late. They'd know something mental was involved and would call in Gommaf. Could you hold them off?"

Gowru shrugged. Rains thought he probably could, though he might not be aware of it yet. But though they'd be safe from the mental onslaught of Gommaf, there was a catch. Sooner or later they'd have to have food and water, the screen would come down and then they'd be at the mercy of the Indian mentalists.

There had to be another way and he thought he saw it. "How long can you keep this up?"

"For days," sat Gowru. "Once it's in existence I merely have to touch it now and then to keep it up."

"Good. Make a small hole so you can see where you're going and start out across the plain." It was late afternoon and would soon be dark....

"There's an army camp ahead," said Gowru.

"National guard?"

"Multi-national guard. This is India."

Rains sighed. There was no use asking what was on either side and behind them—more troops. Planes droned overhead. Mobile searchlights were trained on them. Fortunately, there were no big guns in this area. Perhaps Gowru could build up the image to withstand even the direct hit of a large caliber shell, but the concussion wouldn't be pleasant. "If there's an army camp there must be a trench," Rains said. "Do you see any?"

Gowru Chandit looked. "There's a trench."

"Angle the tank so we'll pass directly over it." He paused. "Can you project this image?"

"Keep it in existence and control where it goes though we're no longer inside? Yes, I can do that."

"Fine. And can you make a hole in the bottom as the tank shape passes over the trench?"

"I can."

"That's what I thought. My idea is that we drop into the trench and the tank continues on. It goes into the forest beyond the camp and as soon as all the troops have followed, you destroy the image."

"Instantly?"

"If you can."

Gowru breathed gustily. "I can create it instantly, but the reverse is not true. It has to fade away, and that takes time."

Rains didn't want that, since it would reveal the nature of the tank. "Is there any other way to dispose of it?"

"I think so," said Gowru. "I can project it into the forest and let it rise later with a trail of fire. I can imitate a rocket."

A rocket tank would give them something to think about. "Excellent. But remember to drop out of sight in the trench. The troops on foot will be concerned with the tank. They won't notice us in the darkness."

Gowru nodded and they went on. Presently he spoke. "Here we are."

They dropped. The trench was deep and it was near a swamp. They fell into half a foot of water. Overhead, the troops marched away.

They fell into half a foot of water, while overhead, troops were marching.

Gowru straightened and looked out. He climbed up and extended his hand, pulling Rains to the top.

As they stood there, a trail of fire rose over the forest, the tank image bursting upward and disappearing. It was too soon. The troops wouldn't find anything though they'd scour around. They'd have to return. Rains was aching to empty his shoes of cold water.

Together they started out, slinking through the deserted camp. They hurried, but they didn't have much leeway. Soldiers began straggling back. There was no time to look for a trail through the swamp, if there was a trail.

They crashed through a dense fringe of vines and fell into the swamp. They had been wet, now they became drenched. Mud clung to them, sticky, foul-smelling slime. Rains could imagine snakes and unspeakable vermin crawling away from them or toward them as they crashed onward. Branches slashed at them, mud sucked them down. Gasping, they floundered away.

Anyone could follow their trail. But no one was likely to associate such bedraggled men with the phenomenon that had lately puzzled the best minds of the Indian army....

Rains was awakened by a rhythmical thud nearby. He jumped up and looked around and then relaxed. It was Gowru pounding clothing on a flat rock in a pool of brackish water. He had pulverized a native plant and added it to the water, producing a reasonable imitation of soap.

Rains wrinkled his nose in disgust. The stench still clung to his body in spite of attempts to wash it off last night before falling asleep. Silently, Gowru gave him some of the soap plant, and he found another pool to bathe in. He emerged feeling much cleaner.

The Hindu had spread the clothing to dry in the clearing. Rains lay down and let the warm sun soak into his bones, pondering. They had no food and couldn't expect to find much in the swamp. And after last night there'd be soldiers around, combing the area, looking for an explanation of the mysterious tank. Now he couldn't expect to enter the Gommaf building undetected from the rear. They'd have to get back to the road that led to the city and from there return to the hotel. Afterwards, they'd have to plan anew. But for the moment, raw survival was paramount.

The clothing soon dried. Dressed, the Hindu looked presentable, but that was because his garments were exceedingly simple. The Western synthetic fabric didn't launder well. Sadly, Rains looked at his reflection in the water. He was rumpled.

They started in the direction they imagined the road lay, staying within the cover at the edge of the swamp. On the plain there were light tanks and armored vehicles, battalions of soldiers, planes circling overhead.

Weary and hungry they struggled for hours through the swamp. At last the wilderness ended. They crouched in the underbrush where the trees stopped and gazed at a building, the front of which faced the road they sought. It was a queer structure, a small-scale skyscraper with chrome plated carvings.

If they could get to the building and then to the highway, they should be safe. To get to the building was hardest. A few hundred yards away platoons of soldiers wheeled in formation. They'd be spotted if they tried to cross the open space.

He sighed. The soldiers might go away, but he couldn't plan on it. What would work—another tank on the plain? It would attract them, all right, but it would also be a signal to mobilize the entire army and put it on guard duty in this area. A sovereign nation didn't want strange tanks inside its borders.

He located the officer in charge of the drill. The sun was hot and the soldiers were perspiring. The lieutenant was not a full-fledged sadist, but he was studying to be one and didn't need much urging. The cadence of command rose sharply. The men turned and began marching out on the open plain.

Rains jabbed Gowru and, crouching low, they began to run toward the building. The distance was greater than he had estimated; he was hungry and short of breath and his mind wandered. He couldn't concentrate and his control of the officer slipped away.

"About face!" screeched the lieutenant, and a half-hundred men were staring at the fugitives.

It was too late to reach the road, but in the building lay temporary safety. Rains dived over the low wall and Gowru followed. He ran across the garden and, reaching a window, tore it open and climbed inside, pulling the Hindu up after him.

As he turned to help, he stared in amazement at the soldiers. The officer was blowing his whistle and shouting into the field radio, but his men, who had darted after the fugitives, had stopped at the wall. Gowru nodded and grinned. "Temple," he grunted.

Of course. With so many nationalities and divergent beliefs, the government had granted immunity from search to those religions, sects and cults that demanded it. The place was safer than he thought. He grabbed the Hindu's arm. "Down," he said.

Gowru grabbed his arm. "Up," he said. "We've got to see what they're doing." It was logical. Rains reversed his direction.

On his way up the dimly lit tower, Rains collided with someone. From the quality of her robe and jewels and the paint on her face, he placed her as a high priestess of some sort. She smirked at him and beckoned mysteriously; then swayed down the hall, apparently expecting him to follow. Strange behaviour in a temple sanctuary. He shook his head and went on after Gowru.

The Hindu had settled in a luxurious room at the top of the tower and was looking out the window. The temple was surrounded. Not a soldier had entered the grounds, but a solid cordon of armed men hemmed them in. And dust in the distance down the road foretold of more to come. The army wanted them for questioning. How they proposed to get them out of the temple Rains didn't know, but the situation seemed as hopeless as it could get.

With an effort he made his mind slippery and broke contact. A master mentalist was at work. He resisted the impulse to leave the temple and surrender. Tentatively he let his thoughts reach out. No, this was merely a journeyman—the masters were on their way.

He turned in panic to Gowru, who was opening cabinets. Row after row of expensive liquor glittered within. There was little resemblance to a monk's bare cell; the place was more nearly a sybarite's palace. It was a peculiar religion.

Gowru tilted back his head and gurgled. "Want a fog?" he asked. "I've got the raw materials."

A fog wasn't satisfactory. They could elude the soldiers and slip away in the confusion, but they couldn't hope to escape the mentalists. On the other hand, yesterday the tank surface had repelled his own thoughts. It should work.

"Can you put an impenetrable surface around us?"

"Won't work," said Gowru, wiping his lips. "It has to be a closed surface, and if it's strong enough to stop anything it's also strong enough to shear through any material in the way. Up here we'd topple to the ground as soon as a gust of wind came along."

That was an aspect of the shield he hadn't guessed at. He fought frantically for control of his mind. "Then put it around the whole temple, grounds and all. Exclude the soldiers."

Gowru nodded. "I can do that. Within reasonable limits size doesn't mean much, it's the principle that counts. I'll make it a big spherical shield."

Instantly the room became gray, as light from the outside diminished; but most important, the mental tension lessened. Rains looked out. It was difficult to see through the shield, but he could make out dim shapes. The journeyman mentalist tried to get through.

The shield was good, but a new force arrived; the masters were here and added their mental force to that of the journeyman. Rains reeled under the impact. "Make it more intense!" he shouted. "Give it all you've got!"

Gowru grabbed at another bottle and gave it everything. The grayness became blackness and the intruding thoughts of the mentalists, masters and journeyman, disappeared altogether.

He relaxed. Temporarily, they were safe. He felt giddy and his stomach squirmed around. There was no reason for this last effect—none that he could think of....

Rains counted the bottles. It was not an accurate way to determine the passage of time, but there was no electricity and none of the clocks were running. He snapped on the flashlight. How many bottles equalled one day?

He was getting hungry. He'd managed to scrounge some food in the darkness, aided by the flashlight, but it hadn't been enough. On his forays his contacts with the other humans in the temple had been disconcerting. Giggles in the distance and then squeals, but he'd never been able to come upon the source. He didn't blame them for being so wary; the darkness and isolation must seem like something supernatural.

Water was getting low too; only trickles came from the faucet. The shield had severed all contact with the outside world, including plumbing connections, and only a tank and a pressure system inside the temple had kept them going this long.

He'd have to risk a look, perhaps the vigilance outside had been relaxed. He shook the guide. Gowru grunted and stretched out his hand. Rains shoved a half empty bottle in it; he had to conserve. The supply of liquor was getting low, at least in this room. "Can you put a hole in the shield, a small one?"

Gowru raised the bottle and later set it down. "Nope. Takes too much thinking. How about a transparent area?"

"That will do."

Gowru staggered to the window, leaned on the sill and stared out. He stared longer than Rains expected him to. "So that's what happened to it," he muttered. He groped for a chair and sat down, shaking with laughter.

It couldn't be that funny, decided Rains, going to the window. He peered out and it was dark. Gowru had neglected to clear an area to see through. No, there were dots of light outside—it was night, that's all.

That was not all. Very near, as astronomical distances go, and headed toward them, was a comet. Not a comet, *the* comet.

Rains sat down before he grew dizzy. What was the comet doing so close, unless they were out in space? He opened his eyes and looked again. That's where they were. Unless he was mistaken, that was Mars over there.

He tried to fit the facts together. It made sense, but offered no hope. He had proof that the shield was adjustable—stronger or weaker. As it was made progressively stronger, it shut out light, bullets, and thoughts. Could it be made strong enough to shut out gravity?

He looked outside. It could.

Gowru had exerted himself and the shield had sliced through earth, water and sewer connections. Centrifugal force and the motion of the solar system through space accounted for their present position. The temple had whizzed away from the face of Earth before the astonished eyes of the Indian Army.

Gowru was still laughing. He clapped Rains heartily on the back. "So that's where it went," he said.

"Where what went?" asked Rains. They were doomed to be flung into outer space and nothing could save them.

"The Benares cremation barge. It floated to the comet."

Float was hardly the word for the intricate process that had taken place. Rains could see the comet, and he had known all along that the barge was on it.

"What do you know about the cremation barge?" he asked.

Gowru fondled the bottle. "One day I was swimming in the Ganges and an alligator—"

"There are no alligators in India."

Gowru Chandit gestured in defeat. "If you must know, I didn't have a job and each night I swam out to the barge to sleep. I slept late one morning and the crew found me and tossed me off. I had to swim in."

"But you always swam in anyway."

"Makes no difference," said Gowru. "So, when they left that night, I projected a shield around the barge. Come to think of it, it was probably like the one I've got around the temple. Anyway, in the morning the barge had disappeared and no one, including me, knew where it went—until now. The city had to buy another one to replace it."

Rains looked at him dazedly. That's what he'd seen in the psiscope—the barge—and it was for this reason he'd come to Benares. But it wasn't a teleport that was responsible; it was his own guide, Gowru Chandit. Gowru hadn't known because he hadn't told him.

There were other aspects. "After the shield is created it dies down?"

"It does, unless I renew it."

The barge had drifted away from Earth like the temple, and then the shield had disintegrated in such a way as to leave the barge subject to the gravitational field of the comet which had then captured it.

"Can you alter the shield at will so that one side is affected by gravity and the other not?"

Gowru Chandit, dyeman extraordinary, saw what the question was aimed at. He scratched his head. "Can I, by varying the strength of the field, take us to Mars? I think I can."

An astronomer's dream! While his colleagues were merely looking at it, Rains would be on Mars! It would take cunning work by the Hindu, but if Gowru said he could do it, Rains couldn't disbelieve. There was one drawback though, and that reflected on his face.

"There's no water and little air on Mars," said Rains. "We'll reach it, but we'll die soon after."

"Hmmm," said Gowru. Coming from anyone else it would not have been a profound comment. He got unsteadily to his feet and paced around the room, gathering bottles as he went. He squinted out the window. "The very fabric of space," he muttered. He seemed to be looking at the comet.

He beckoned to Rains. "Come here." He had enough liquor inside and he really didn't need what he held in his hands, except perhaps he liked the feel of bottles. "Look," he said, and pointed. Rains looked.

There was the comet, streaming away from the sun, headed in the direction of Mars, though it would miss by several million miles. He'd seen it before.

But, somewhere in space it struck something. There was nothing there, but it broke into tiny fragments and slanted toward Mars. There was no doubt that Mars was going to capture most of the mass, and would soon have an abundance of water and oxygen.

But there was nothing for the comet to strike! Except—Except what? "The very fabric of space," Gowru had muttered, and that proved merely that he was a poor semanticist. The *structure* of space. That's what he worked with, not molecules, though he didn't know it. Gowru had projected a space warp inclined chutelike toward Mars, and when the comet came along it had collided with a plane surface anchored to the entire universe.

Water, air, and a new planet to explore, with Gowru Chandit as his companion. But there was still one last defect. He groaned aloud.

"Is there something else to complain about?" asked Gowru.

Rains gestured savagely to indicate the whole temple. "I'm a man of science," he said bitterly. "I resent being marooned with religious fanatics."

"Don't worry. They're women."

That made it worse. Monks, or the Indian equivalent, he could ignore. But could he do the same with grim and dour females intent on saving his soul?

Just the same, they were going to be on Mars with him and in self-defence he'd have to learn their religion, the better to refute it. "What are the fine points of their theology?" he asked.

"Very old," muttered Gowru. "Priestesses are selected for temperamental qualifications. Rites are ancient Hindu, maybe older than that."

"Rites?" he queried. "Sacrifices?"

"It's no sacrifice," yawned the other. "They're a local fertility cult."

Rains' mind swung back to the priestess he had encountered on first entering the temple, the only one he'd seen. The hall had been dimly lighted, but she'd been young and very seductive. If the others were like her—Any scientist worth his salt believed in fertility, one way or another.

Milton Keynes UK
Ingram Content Group UK Ltd.
UKHW010628080324
438959UK00005B/367